A Gopher's Christmas Adventure

Pierre Fiset and Damiano Ferraro

Published by FlowerPublish

ISBN: 978-1-989277-86-7

Flowerpublish
www.flowerpublish.com
Montreal, Canada

To our friends, families and leafy green vegetables.
Thanks to you, you've allowed us to create our gopher adventures and share them with others.

First of all, what is a gopher? A gopher is a little animal that can be found almost all over the world. There are many kinds of gophers, but most of them have two little ears, a cute little nose and two big teeth for nibbling their food. They like vegetables very much. With their powerful claws they can dig and they really love to dig. They can dig long and deep tunnels underground. Not many people know what their lives are like because they are secretive and shy little creatures. What kind of adventures do they have? Maybe one of their adventures could be like this:

nce below a time...

...in
   a
     land
       far
         beneath
           ours...

Toby and Oliver were writing their letters to Santa Gopher, in Miss Topsoil's class.

It was the last day before the Christmas vacation.

Oliver raised his paw to ask his teacher a question.

"Are you sure our letters will reach Santa Miss Topsoil?" he asked.

Oliver had been especially good this year and he really wanted to give Santa Gopher enough time to make all his presents.

"Don't worry Oliver," replied Miss Topsoil, "the letters will get there in time. Just bring it home and give it to your mom and dad and they will mail it for you."

After school, Toby went to Oliver's burrow to play. Toby was Oliver's best friend. They had been friends since they were very young gophers.

"Toby, I don't think Miss Topsoil was right." said Oliver. "I'm not so sure Santa will get the Christmas list in time. Last year I only got half the presents I wanted!"

"Toby, I'm going to bring my list to Santa myself," said Oliver. "Do you want to come with me?"

"Ok, Oliver," said Toby "but we have to plan our trip before we go. Do you know where Santa's workshop is?"

"No," answered Oliver, "but I bet you three carrots that Rupert Rutabaga knows where to go."

They went to see Rupert, the plumpest yet smartest gopher in Miss Topsoil's class. Rupert was in his backyard, looking through his vegiescope, a telescope specially made to look at vegetables.

He was admiring the onion bulbs in the cavern ceiling.

"Sorry to bother you, Rupert," said Oliver, "but do you know where Santa Gopher's workshop is?"

"That is a tricky question," said Rupert, "but I think I know where it is."

Rupert took them to his bedhole and pulled out a map of the world from his book of maps. The map showed all the gopher autoroots from Walnutville, the town they lived in. The autoroots went in four main directions: N, S, E and W.

"I think the S stands for Santa so this is the autoroot you should take," Rupert said tracing his finger down the map. "The E stands for the Easter Bunny, I think the N stands for Nothing Much, But Ice and of course the W stands for Wally the Wooly Walruses' Wonderful Wacky Waterworks."

"Are you sure the S stands for Santa? Shouldn't you look it up in a book?" asked Oliver.

"I'm very sure," answered Rupert, "but I doubt you will find him without my help."

Oliver decided to trust Rupert because he was right most of the time and knew a lot of things that Oliver didn't know.

"Would you like to come see Santa with us?" asked Oliver.

"Of course," answered Rupert, "it would be very interesting."

"Can I come too?" said someone behind the door. "Pretty please with spinach on top." It was Rudolph, Rupert's younger brother. He had been listening to the older gophers from behind Rupert's door.

"Sure," said Oliver.

Rupert frowned at his little brother.

"Well I suppose I could use some help with the maps and also the Vegetable Positioning System (V.P.S.)." said Rupert hesitantly.

A V.P.S. is something that gophers use to help them find out where they are on a map and to help them find vegetables.

"We have to ask our mother first," said Rupert.

They went to see Rodentia Rutabaga, Rupert and Rudolph's mother. Little gophers can leave their homes to take adventures, but they always tell their parents first. Mrs. Rutabaga agreed and she promised to make some sandwiches for them.

Toby went home and told his parents he was going on a trip with Oliver. He went to his room and packed his shovel and pick, his sleeping bag, his toothbrush and some vegetables.

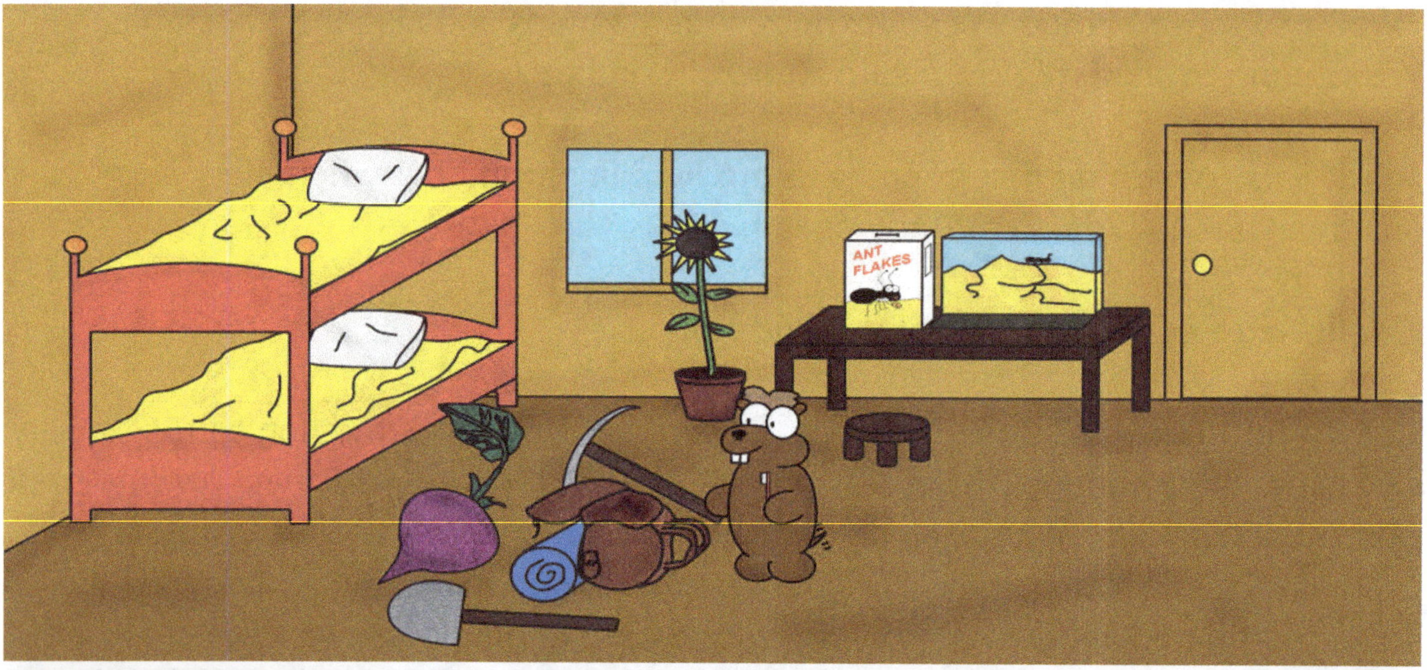
ANT FLAKES

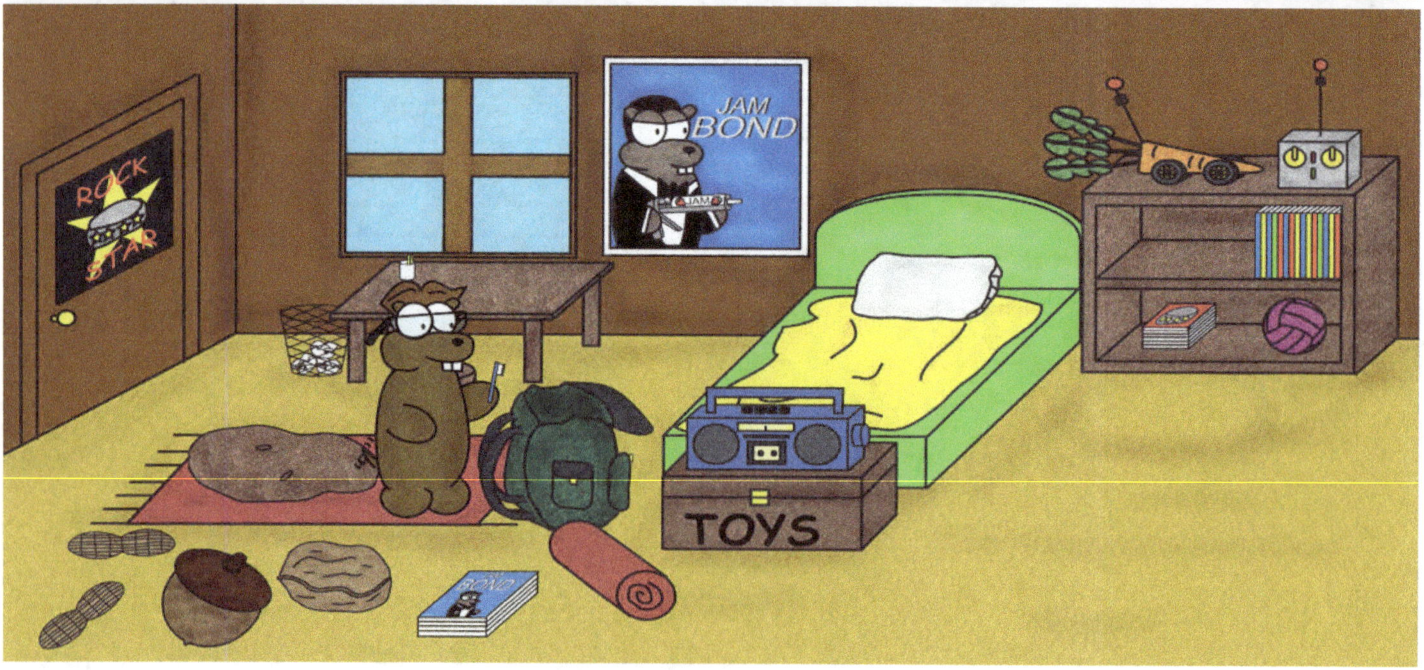
ROCK STAR
JAM BOND
JAM
TOYS

Oliver went home and told his parents that he was going on a trip, but would be home for Christmas. He went to his room and packed his sleeping bag, his toothbrush, some roots and nuts and some comic books for the trip. Oliver loved comic books and his favorites were the Jam Bond Super Secret Spy books.

Rupert left the kitchen and went back to his bedhole with Rudolph. He finally decided that he only needed one raincoat, his safari hat, his safari clothes, a walking stick, a warm coat, a warm hat, a telescope, his microvegescope, his V.P.S., his drawing table, one set of his special map-writing pencils, his flashlight, his camera and some travel books.

Rudolph was going to bring the tent, the food, the tools, the maps, parts of the V.P.S. that Rupert couldn't carry and the toothbrushes.

The gopher boys met up in front of Oliver's burrow and when they made sure they had everything they needed, including their toothbrushes, they set off.

A few days passed and the gophers followed Rupert as he guided them towards where he thought Santa lived.

"The map says there is a big corn field over our heads," said Rupert, "Let's get some corn. Oliver and Toby go up from the tunnel, while Rudolph and I study the map."

Rupert unfolded his portable map table, took out the map and his pencils while Rudolph tried to help.

"I guess we don't have much choice," said Oliver to Toby, "Let's go get the corn. It will be nice to go to the surface. It's getting warmer and warmer in this tunnel."

Oliver took a shovel and dug up to the surface. Oliver sniffed the air. Something smelled funny, but he didn't know what it was. He got out of the hole and went to get a cob of corn.

All of a sudden, a large snake appeared from the corn stalks. It was about to pounce on the gophers.

"Quick Toby, do something," cried Oliver as he ran away from the snake.

While Oliver ran away to hide, Toby pulled a beet out of his pack and flung it at the snake. The beet hit the snake's head and it slithered away.

"That was close," said Oliver hurrying back. "Thanks for taking care of that snake, Toby."

"You sure gave that snake quite a beeting." someone said behind them in a delightful Spanish accent.

Surprised that somebody had been watching them, Oliver and Toby turned around. On the edge of the cornfield, calmly nibbling a piece of asparagus was another young gopher about their age, wearing a sombrero and a poncho.

After introducing themselves, Oliver and Toby explained to Enrico that they were seeking Santa Gopher. Enrico explained to them that they were going the wrong way and that "S" meant South not Santa. He told them that "N" stood for North and that Santa Gopher lived at the North Pole.

Oliver and Toby asked Enrico if he wanted to help them find Santa Gopher.

"Ok," said Enrico. "I'll go ask my parents."

While Enrico went to ask his parents, Oliver and Toby collected some corn for their trip. Enrico, soon came back. His parents had agreed. After the trip Enrico was going to meet his parents at his grandmother's burrow in Chestnutville which was quite close to Walnutville, the city Oliver and Toby were from.

They hopped back into the tunnel and found Rupert drawing on the map.

"I'm Rupert and this is my brother Rudolph. Who are you?" asked Rupert curiously.

"I am Enrico, son of Pablo, the greatest nibbler in the South," said Enrico with his delightful Spanish accent, "and you must be the potato head that told them that Santa lives in the South."

"Yes, I, wait a minute I . . ." mumbled Rupert

Oliver and Toby explained to Rupert and Rudolph that they had been going the wrong way. They also told them that Enrico was going to help them to see Santa Gopher.

Enrico had the map now because he knew which autoroots they should take to get to the North Pole. Rupert was a little angry, but he quickly found out that Enrico was very good with the map.

As they travelled north, they passed by a huge underground city.
"What city do you suppose that is, Toby?" asked Oliver.

"I don't know. It's the biggest city I've ever seen," said Toby. "Do you know what city it is Rupert?"

"Are both of you guys kidding?" exclaimed Rupert. "That's the Big Apple. The one and only New Fork City. My aunt lives there next to the Central Park. Next time Rudolph and I go see my aunt, you three should come visit. There are so many things to do and see in New Fork."

They didn't have time to stop and visit because they had to get to the North Pole. They had already taken too much time by going south instead of north.

As they walked, Oliver told his friends of the many great things he wanted to ask Santa Gopher to bring him for Christmas. He wanted many things including an iPawd, the official Rock Star™ action figures, a Vegestation vegetable entertainment system with games, many comic books and many other things.

"I hope Santa can bring me all of these things," said Oliver.

"You asked for a lot things, Oliver," said Toby. "I didn't want that much for Christmas."

"I agree with Toby," said Enrico, "Christmas isn't really about presents, it is about spending time with your family and friends."

After several more days, the gophers came to a construction sign that was in the middle of the autoroot and blocking the way. On the sign it said that the tunnel ahead was flooded. The stream had leaked into the tunnel and the following stretch of autoroot was under construction.

"What do we do?" asked Rudolph. "How will we get to Santa Gopher?"

"There's another autoroot we can take to go north," said Enrico, in a delightful Spanish accent, "but it will take time. We will need to hurry to make it to the North Pole and then back again in time for Christmas."

So they took the autoroots that Enrico suggested. After many days of walking, they found that their autoroot was getting colder.

Rupert put on his warm jacket. The other gophers had not brought any clothing with them so they were a little jealous of Rupert. Rudolph was especially cold until Rupert lent him his warm hat.

Enrico wanted to know why the tunnel had gotten so cold. Enrico started to dig upwards, but needed Toby's pick because the ground was too hard for his claws.

As he reached the top, a heap of snow came crashing down on the gophers. After digging their way out of the cold powdery snow, Enrico climbed to the top of the hole and looked outside to see where they were.

At the surface, there was a large elk. Enrico stared at the huge and mighty creature. The elk sniffed the small helpless rodent.

"Say, big fella, do you know where we can find Santa Gopher?" Enrico asked with his delightful Spanish accent.

The elk grunted, disappointed that he couldn't eat the gopher and walked away. Enrico was surprised at how rude the elk was and went back into the tunnel.

The gophers continued their search, following the map until the end of the autoroot. The five adventurers decided to go up to the surface to see if they could get some help from a more polite animal.

On the surface was a mighty big surprise.

"Mighty Jalapeños!" cried Enrico.

"Great beans of India!" exclaimed Oliver.

"Great Gopherstein's ghost!" said Rupert.

"It's . . . it's . . . it's," Toby couldn't let out the words.

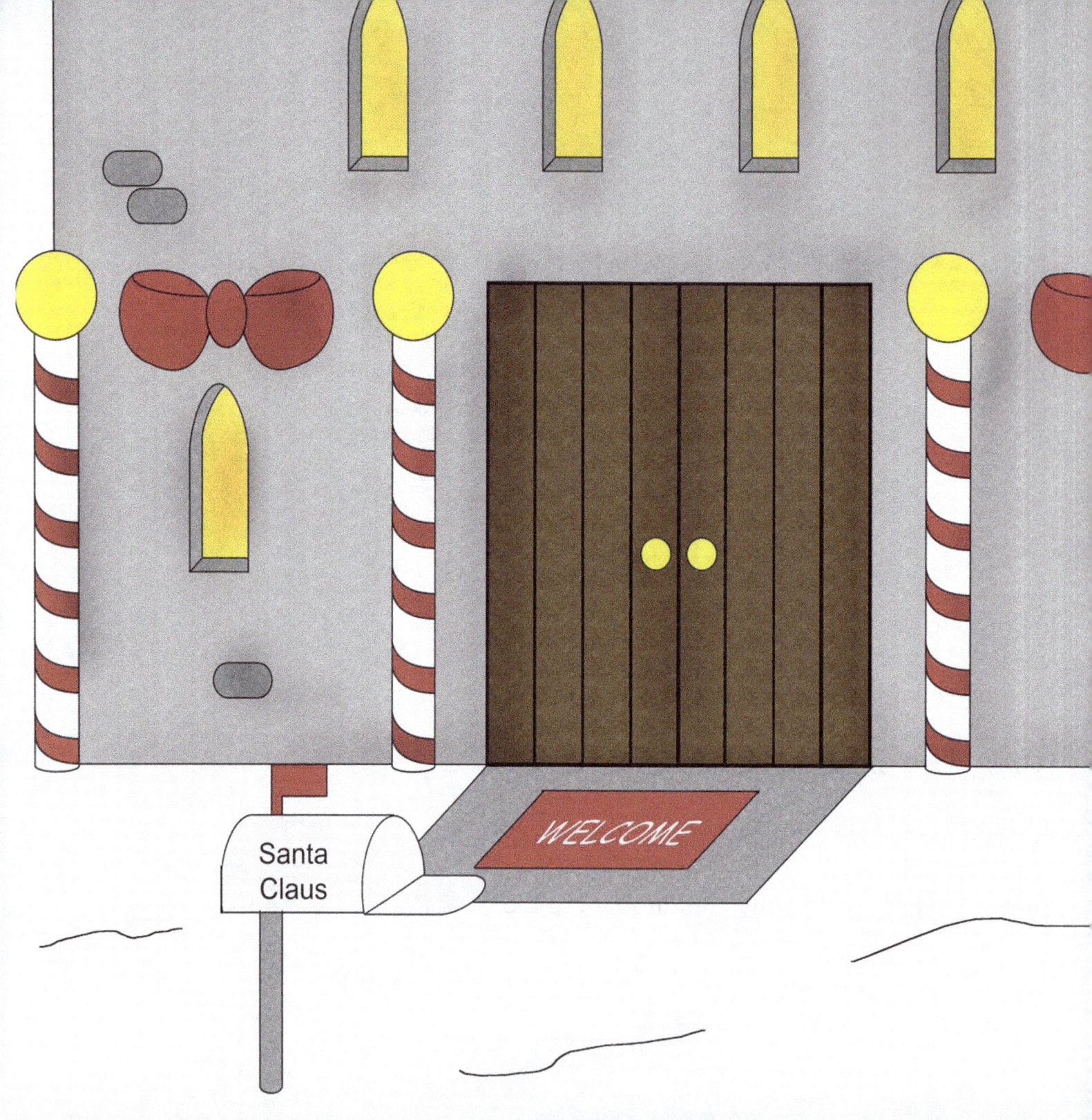

"Santa's Workshop!" cried Rudolph.

They had found it. It was a little burrow next to Santa Claus' castle. Santa Gopher was Santa Claus' neighbor. They went up to the door and Rupert knocked. The door opened and a little elfish gopher popped his head out of the workshop.

"Hello," said the little elfish gopher. "Can I help you?"

"We have dug many miles to come see Santa Gopher. Can we speak to him?" asked Oliver.

"Please come in," said the elfish gopher. "It is very cold outside."

They went inside and followed the little gopher down a hole. The hole led down to Santa's underground workshop.

"I will take you to Santa's nibbling room and get you some turnip cookies and lichen tea while you wait," said the elfish gopher.

The little elfish gopher left and came back with the tea and cookies. An older gopher woman was with the elfish gopher.

"Hello, dear little ones," said the woman. "I am Mrs. Santa Gopher."

"My husband finished making his list and he is checking it a second time before the final delivery. I hope you understand that he won't be able to see you. I wish you had come sooner because he would have gladly listened to all your Christmas wishes."

They had come so far and they wouldn't see Santa Gopher! The gopher children became very disappointed.

"Maybe I can make you feel better," said Mrs. Santa Gopher, "Would you boys like to see our workshop before you go?"

They quickly agreed to Mrs. Santa Gopher's suggestion. After warming themselves with the tea, the boys followed Mrs. Santa Gopher to the main workshop.

The workshop was a large underground city with many different buildings. Each building made different things that Santa brings to gophers all over the world.

There were a lot elfish gophers around and everyone looked busy.

Mrs. Santa Gopher took them to of one the train stations and they travelled to the Candy and Cookie building.

The inside of this building smelled wonderful.

It was like a huge kitchen with little elfish gophers stirring bowls, chopping up ingredients and putting things in ovens. At the moment they were making gingerbread gophers.

"All of these recipes are my own," explained Mrs. Santa Gopher.

"Here try some of my gingerbread gophers."

"Splendid," said Rupert. "I believe these are as good as my mother's."

Next, they went to the Board Game, Toy Models and Puzzles building. They had much to see so they didn't stay long enough to try any of the games even though they looked like fun. In the building, little elfish gophers were making jigsaw puzzles of beets.

In the Musical Instruments building, Enrico tried one of the guitars and Toby tried the drum set. There was also a little gopher orchestra trying out the instruments in a room.

In the next building, the Dolls and Action Figures building, they got to see how the official Rock Star Action figures were made.

They also saw some little elfish gophers making Beetie dolls. Oliver tried one of the new Vegetaforming figurines.

The Cooking Toys building was very interesting. There were all kinds of
utensils and cooking tools for gopher children. There were some tooth made
wooden spoons, spice racks, aprons, hats, pots and pans. Toby saw a set of spoons
with Rudolph's name on them and hid it quickly so Rudolph wouldn't see it.

In the Gardening and Tools building, the elfish gophers were making hammers and pickaxes. Along the wall were some shovels. Toby was able to try a Vegematix 5000, a shovel he had dreamed of trying for a long time.

In the Clothes building, gopher tailors were making coats. There was also an older elfish gopher knitting some socks. Mrs. Santa Gopher explained that most of the time parents would ask for clothing for their kids for Christmas.

In the Books, Magazines and Stationary building, there were more books than in all of Walnutville. Pencils, erasers and crayons were being made there too. Rupert also wanted to stay and read and Oliver found some comic books, but they had to hurry and there were still many things to see and do.

They took the train to the Video Gaming and Electronics building. It was a big building where little elfish gophers were making computers, Vegestation entertainment systems and other electronic toys. Oliver got to try out the Super Potato game with Enrico.

After the Video Game building, they went to the Packaging and Wrapping building. This was where all the toys were wrapped and put into Santa's bag. Santa's office was also in this building.

Oliver wanted to go see Santa, but there were two elfish gopher guards in front of Santa's door that stopped anybody from going in. Mrs. Santa Gopher also said that Santa didn't want to be disturbed.

They left the Packaging and Wrapping building to go to the Mail building. There was only one little elfish gopher in the room and he was sweeping the floor with a broom.

"We finished getting Christmas lists for this year," explained Mrs. Santa Gopher. "That's why it is so quiet."

"Mrs. Santa Gopher," said Oliver, "we came to visit Santa Gopher so I could give him my list in person, but we came too late. Does that mean that I won't get anything for Christmas?"

"Don't worry Oliver," said Mrs. Santa Gopher, "Santa Gopher usually brings leftover toys and some socks. So everybody gets something in the end."

Oliver couldn't believe it. He probably wasn't going to get anything on his list at all.

They went back to the nibbling room and Mrs. Santa Gopher gave them coats, hats and food for their trip home. They thanked Mrs. Santa Gopher for her help and for the tour of the workshop.

They hurried home because there wasn't much time before Christmas. Oliver was very sad and he was worried that he would only get socks for Christmas after all that walking and adventuring.

When they arrived in Walnutville, Enrico hurried to Chestnutville to his grand-mother's burrow where his parents already waited.

Oliver invited Enrico for the big Christmas lunch planned at his burrow and Enrico promised he would be there.

Toby, Oliver, Rupert and Rudolph all went to their homes. When Oliver got home, it was very late and Oliver's parents were already sleeping. He left a note telling his parents he had invited more people to the Christmas lunch and went quietly to his room. After brushing his teeth, Oliver went into his pile of hay.

Oliver fell asleep and he started to dream.

He dreamed it was Christmas morning. He was in the den with his friends and Santa Gopher was giving out presents. Oliver waited for his turn, but soon there were no more presents under the Christmas root.

"Uh-oh," said Santa. "I don't think I have anything for you. I'm sure our friends will find something to do."

The gophers started singing some Christmas songs and Enrico played his guitar. They sang Christmas Root, Deck the Tunnels, Nibble Nuts and many others. After the singing they had Christmas cookies made by Rupert's mom. Oliver's grandfather told some stories. Then they played games. Oliver had so much fun he had forgotten that he hadn't gotten anything for Christmas. He didn't think the fun would end.

Oliver woke up. The singing, the presents, Santa and the cookies had all been a dream.

Oliver got up and went to the dining room and found that his parents and grandfather were already awake. Toby had brought his whole family including his parents, his older brother Toberto, his younger sister Tobina, his younger brother Tobino and his baby brother Toborio. Rupert and Rudolph were also there with their mother Rodentia. Enrico had arrived with his parents and his grandmother from Chestnutville.

"Merry Christmas Oliver!" cried out everyone as he entered the room.

"Merry Christmas to you all!" answered Oliver.

Everybody was about to have lunch, but they were waiting for Oliver to join in.

After their meal, they all went to the Christmas root and opened their presents. Oliver couldn't believe it, though there were some presents under the root for him.

Oliver got a gigantic potato peeler, Ranch Salad Dressing, some socks and many other presents, but he didn't get everything on his list.

He was still happy. He had a great adventure, made a new friend and saw many new things. He also learnt that Christmas was about being with those you loved and showing that you care about them.

Oliver and his friends played with their new presents under the Christmas root until it was time for supper.

THE END
MERRY
CHRISTMAS

Gingerbread gopher recipe:

Get your parents to help you make this tasty recipe. They will need to help you because you will have to use the stove and oven. If you can't find a gopher cookie cutter, you can use a teddy bear cookie cutter instead. These can be found in many stores or online.

1/2 cup (125 mL) of unsalted butter
1/2 cup (125 mL) of packed brown sugar
1 egg
1/2 cup (125 mL) of molasses
1/4 cup (50 mL) of water
2 and 3/4 cups (675 mL) of all purpose flour
1/2 tsp (2 mL) cup of baking soda
1/2 tsp (2 mL) of salt
1 tbsp (15 mL) of ground ginger
1 tsp (5 mL) of cinnamon
1/2 tsp (2 mL) of ground allspice

Directions (Makes about 30-50 gingerbread cookies)

1. In large bowl, cream together butter and brown sugar
2. Beat in egg, molasses and water
3. In a separate bowl, combine the flour, baking soda, salt, ginger, cinnamon and allspice
4. Gradually blend in the flour mixture 1/2 cup at a time until well blended
5. Chill the cookie batter in the refrigerator until firm, for about 30 minutes
6. On a floured surface, roll out dough to 1/8- inch (3 mm) thick
7. Using the cookie cutter, press firmly down to cut out the cookies
8. Place on a cookie sheet lined with parchment paper
9. Bake at 350° F (180° C) oven for 8 to 10 minutes or until just firm
10. Let cool on a wire rack
11. Enjoy!

You can decorate the cookies using cake frosting and candy. Some stores sell many edible decorations like eyes and noses. You can also buy some pens that you can draw on your cookie with edible ink.

Christmas Root (To the tune of O Christmas Tree)

O Christmas Root, O Christmas Root
So brown throughout the seasons,
So brown in summer you do grow
And still as brown under winter's snow.

O Christmas Root, O Christmas Root
So brown throughout the seasons.

O Christmas Root, O Christmas Root
Your dirtiness lasts forever
But most of all at Christmas time.

Your roots so thick bring earth and grime.
O Christmas Root, O Christmas Root
Your dirtiness lasts forever.

O Christmas Root, O Christmas Root
A chore you will give us,
You give delight but soil the room,
And we will have to get the broom.

O Christmas Root, O Christmas Root
A chore you will give us.

Deck the Tunnels (to the tune of Deck The Halls)

Deck the tunnels with bows and ribbons,
Fa la la la la la la la la,

'Tis the season to be givin,
Fa la la la la la la la la,

Wrap we now our loving gift,
Fa la la la la la la la la,

Christmas make your coming swift,
Fa la la la la la la la la,

See the boiling pots before us,
Fa la la la la la la la la,

Stir the soup and clean the lettuce,
Fa la la la la la la la la,

Now we cook our carrots tender,
Fa la la la la la la la la,

And throw them all into the blender.
Fa la la la la la la la la,

Fast away our breakfast passes,
Fa la la la la la la la la,

Dance you gopher lads and lasses,
Fa la la la la la la la la,

Finish off your cake and fruit,
Fa la la la la la la la la,

Gather round our Christmas root.
Fa la la la la la la la la

Nibble Nuts (To the tune of Jingle Bells)

Eating under snow,
In tunnels filled with hay.

Under the fields we go,
Munching all the way.

The nuts in our packs crack,
Making hunger bite,
Oh what fun it is to nibble a tasty nut tonight.

Chorus:
Nibble Nuts, Nibble Nuts
Nibble all the way,
Oh what fun it is to nibble nuts in tunnels filled with hay.